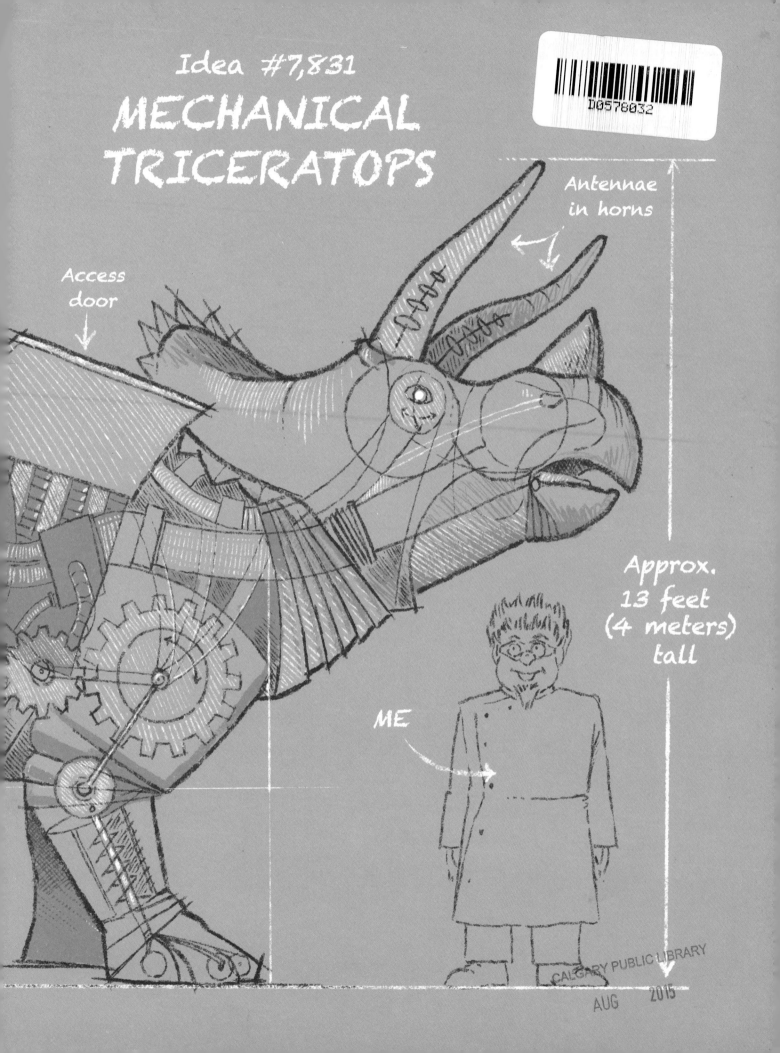

MAD SCIENTIST
ACADEMY

MAD SCIENTIST
ACADEMY
WELCOME NEW STUDENTS!

THE DINOSAUR DISASTER

MATTHEW McELLIGOTT

CROWN BOOKS
FOR YOUNG READERS
NEW YORK

To Christy and Anthony, and to all the hardworking, underappreciated teachers out there. Stay strong!

ACKNOWLEDGMENTS
Dino-sized thanks to Carl Mehling, senior scientific assistant
at the American Museum of Natural History, for his invaluable
guidance and keen eye for detail

Visit us on the Web! randomhousekids.com

Educators and librarians, for a variety of teaching tools, visit us at RHTeachersLibrarians.com

Library of Congress Cataloging-in-Publication Data
McElligott, Matthew, author.
The dinosaur disaster / Matthew McElligott. — First edition.
pages cm. — (Mad Scientist Academy)
Summary: "Dr. Cosmic's class of clever monsters at the Mad Scientist Academy solve the greatest challenges in science,
in this perfect blend of adventure and exploration." —Provided by publisher.
Audience: Ages 5–8.
Audience: K to grade 3.
ISBN 978-0-553-52374-4 (trade) — ISBN 978-0-553-52375-1 (lib. bdg.) — ISBN 978-0-553-52377-5 (ebook)
1. Dinosaurs—Juvenile literature. I. Title.
QE861.5.M383 2015 567.9—dc23 2014039458

The text of this book is set in Sunshine.
The illustrations were created with ink, pencil,
and digital techniques.

MANUFACTURED IN CHINA
10 9 8 7 6 5 4 3 2 1
First Edition

On a cool September morning, a group of students arrive for the first day at their new school....

WHAT IS A PTEROSAUR?

Pterosaurs have been called "flying dinosaurs," but they are not dinosaurs. They are a separate group of flying reptiles that lived among dinosaurs.

Pterosaurs lived during the Triassic, Jurassic, and Cretaceous Periods. Some were only a few inches long. The largest pterosaur ever was the size of a small airplane.

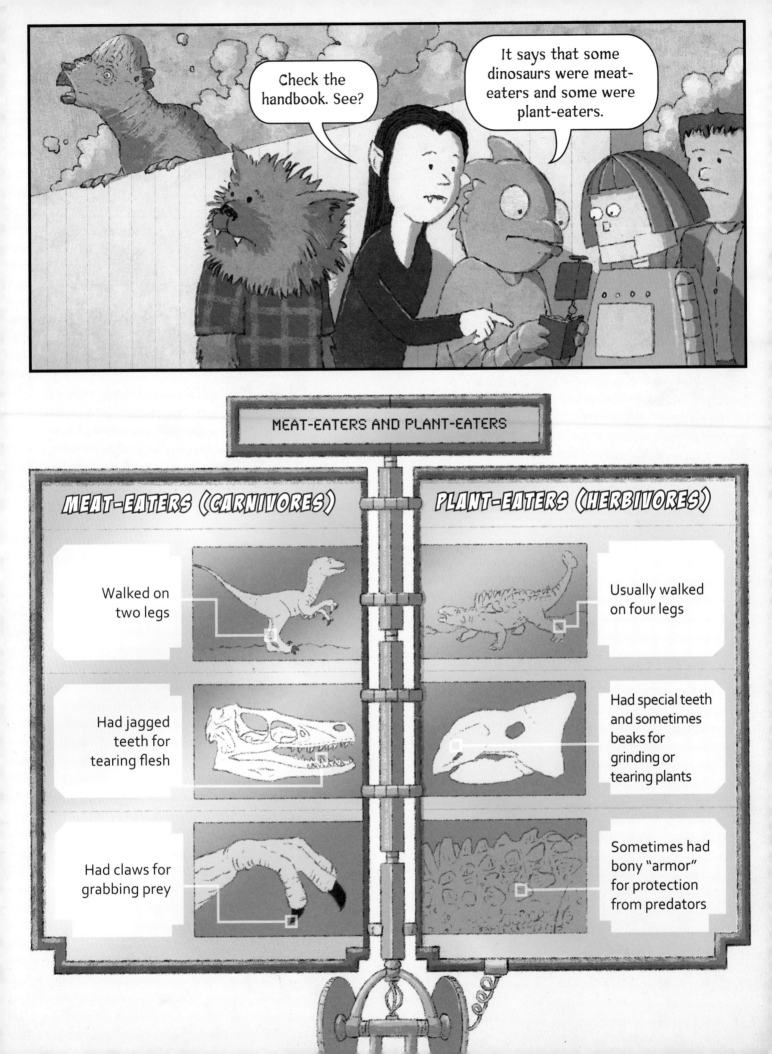

I know this one! Quick! What does the handbook say about *Tyrannosaurus*?

TYRANNOSAURUS REX

SIZE

T. rex was longer than a school bus and as tall as a house, but its arms were only about 3 feet long.

SENSES

T. rex had good vision and an excellent sense of smell, which it used to find live and dead animals to eat.

TAIL

T. rex's large tail helped it balance and make quick turns when it was running.

MOVEMENT

Like most dinosaurs, *T. rex* walked on its toes. Scientists believe it ran about 15 miles per hour.

STEGOSAURUS

A PLANT—EATER, IT HAD SPIKES ON ITS TAIL THAT IT PROBABLY USED FOR DEFENSE.

TRICERATOPS

LIVED IN THE SAME REGIONS AS *TYRANNOSAURUS*. THERE IS EVIDENCE *TYRANNOSAURUS* ATE *TRICERATOPS*. (BE SURE TO KEEP THESE TWO APART!)

ANKYLOSAURUS

HAD HUGE PLATES OF BONE EMBEDDED INTO ITS SKIN AND A BONY CLUB ON ITS TAIL TO KEEP AWAY PREDATORS.

TYRANNOSAURUS REX

ITS JAW WAS 4 FEET LONG (1.2 METERS). IT IS BELIEVED TO HAVE HAD THE MOST POWERFUL BITE OF ANY LAND ANIMAL EVER.

IGUANODON

WHEN ITS SKELETON WAS FIRST DISCOVERED, THE THUMB SPIKE WAS THOUGHT TO BE A HORN ON ITS NOSE.

SPINOSAURUS

WITH A LENGTH OF 50 FEET (15 METERS), IT WAS THE LARGEST KNOWN LAND PREDATOR, BUT ALSO SWAM IN RIVERS TO CATCH FISH.

BRACHIOSAURUS

WEIGHED AS MUCH AS 20 ELEPHANTS AND WAS ABOUT EIGHT STORIES TALL. (WE WILL NEED A HIGH CEILING FOR THIS ONE.)

PACHYCEPHALOSAURUS

ITS SKULL WAS UP TO 9 INCHES (23 CENTIMETERS) THICK AND MAY HAVE BEEN USED TO HEAD—BUTT OTHER ANIMALS.

PARASAUROLOPHUS

THE HOLLOW, BONY CREST ON ITS HEAD WAS LIKELY USED TO MAKE LOUD SOUNDS TO COMMUNICATE.

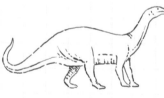

PLATEOSAURUS

LIKELY LIVED IN LARGE HERDS, SINCE FOSSILS OF MANY PLATEOSAURS HAVE BEEN FOUND TOGETHER.

PTEROSAUR

A COUSIN TO DINOSAURS. MOST KNOWN PTEROSAURS LIVED NEAR OCEANS AND SWOOPED OVER THE WATER TO CATCH FISH.

VELOCIRAPTOR

USED THE LARGE, CURVED CLAWS ON EACH BACK FOOT TO HOLD AND KILL THE SMALL DINOSAURS AND OTHER REPTILES THAT IT ATE. (KEEP AN EYE ON THIS ONE— IT COULD MAKE TROUBLE.)

APATOSAURUS

HAD A VERY LONG TAIL, WHICH IT MAY HAVE SNAPPED LIKE A WHIP FOR SELF—DEFENSE OR TO MAKE A LOUD SOUND.

For more dinosaur facts, links, projects, and games, be sure to visit madscientistacademybooks.com.

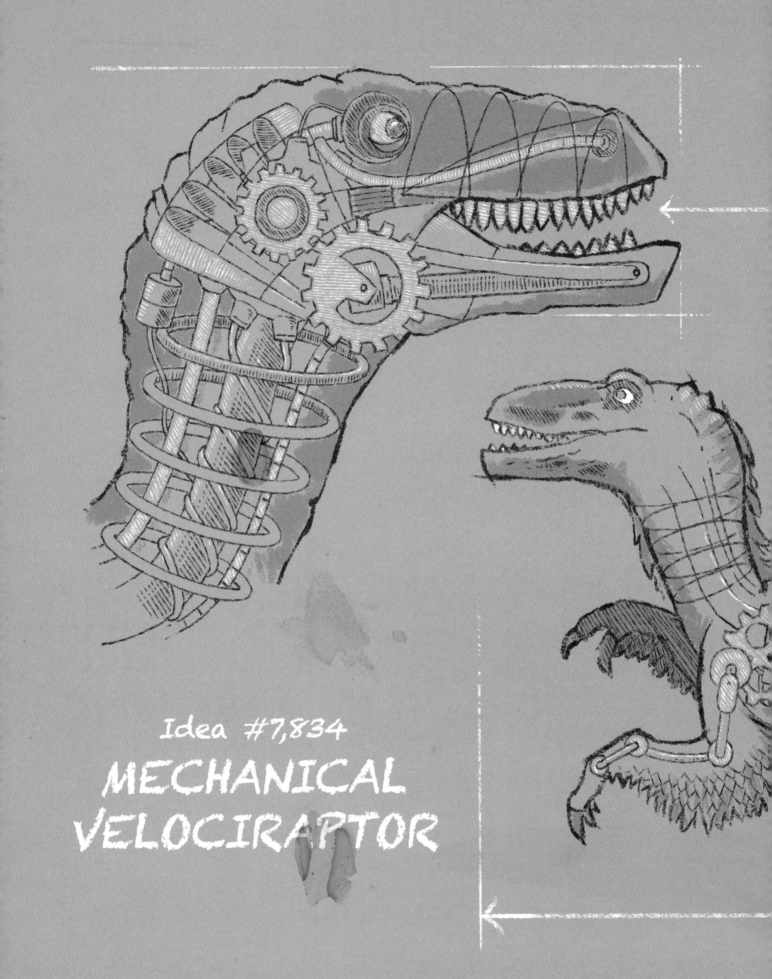

Idea #7,834
MECHANICAL
VELOCIRAPTOR